D1460713

Little Dorrit

Adapted by
Mary Sebag-Montefiore

Illustrated by Barry Ablett

Reading consultant: Alison Kelly
Roehampton University

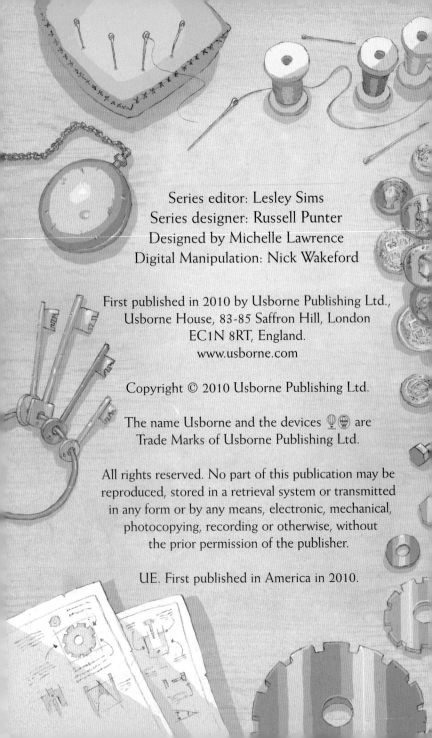

Series editor: Lesley Sims
Series designer: Russell Punter
Designed by Michelle Lawrence
Digital Manipulation: Nick Wakeford

First published in 2010 by Usborne Publishing Ltd.,
Usborne House, 83-85 Saffron Hill, London
EC1N 8RT, England.
www.usborne.com

UE. First published in America in 2010.

Contents

Part One: Poverty

Chapter 1

Born in prison

Sunday evening in London. Nothing to see but streets, streets, streets. Nothing to breathe but streets, streets, streets. One after another, church bells began to clang, slow and fast, maddening, jarring, harsh.

The Marshalsea Prison stood in the borough of Southwark, an oblong barracks of a building with a paved yard in the middle and high walls around – a debtor's prison. If you owed your creditors money, the Marshalsea door swallowed you up with a twist of an iron key. And though your family could join you, free as air to come and go as they pleased, there you were stuck until you paid your debts.

William Dorrit, a new debtor, was worried about his wife. "To give birth in prison," he moaned. "Not what she expected, when she married me…"

"There, there," comforted Bob Chivery, the jailor. "She'll be fine. This place swarms with children. How many have you got already?"

"Two, a boy and a girl. Tip and Fanny."

Bob quickly summed him up – a mild, helpless sort of man with a trembling lip. *And you're another child,* he thought to himself. *That makes three. You look too much of a fool ever to get out of here.*

The new baby was a girl they named Amy. Soon after her birth, Mrs. Dorrit died. The shame of prison depressed her, lowering her will to live.

To Amy, the Marshalsea was not shameful; it was home. Though nobody explained why, she noticed that her father never left his room, while she and Tip and Fanny could play all over the prison. She didn't say anything, but she pitied her father.

Bob saw her pitiful look. "Thinking about the fields, are you, Little Dorrit?"

"What are fields?" Amy asked.

"Why, they're over there," Bob said, waving his key to the distance.

"Are they locked too?"

"Well, not generally. They're full of flowers, buttercups, daisies…"

"Was Father ever there?"

"Have some toffee," offered Bob, changing the subject. But after that, on alternate Sunday afternoons, he took her for walks with his son, John. Amy picked armfuls of flowers to brighten her father's room. Now she realized what he was missing, she pitied him more than ever.

I've got to look after him, she thought. And the others too. Fanny loves dancing. Tip should be in school. Father can't help them, but I *must* do something.

She didn't know why she felt so responsible for her family. The feeling overwhelmed her, as vital as breath. So she dreamed up a plan and the next day she visited one of the prisoners, a dressmaker.

"Please, ma'am, will you teach me needlework?"

"You're very small," said the dressmaker, looking her up and down.

"I know. But I'm willing and eager. Oh, please," Amy begged.

The dressmaker was a generous woman. "I'll teach you everything I know," she said, at last.

Amy was quick to learn, and soon earned money by mending prisoners' clothes. When she'd collected a sizeable sum, she found a school for Tip and a dancing master for Fanny.

Fifteen years later, Mr. Dorrit was the longest-serving inmate the prison had ever known.

"They call me," he said with pride, one evening, "the Father of the Marshalsea. I have given you children a certain status. All visitors here wish to see me. Most slip, discreetly, a welcome coin into my hand. I am a gentleman debtor. I have a position here – the Father of the Marshalsea."

"Yes, Father dear," Amy said, her heart swelling with love and protectiveness.

"You seem to come and go a lot," he added. "Where to, Amy? Not to work, I trust? I couldn't stand the shame if you worked like a servant. You're a lady born and bred."

"Only to see a friend," Amy lied.

By now, she had a daily job as sewing maid to Mrs. Clennam who lived nearby. Her wages paid for treats for her family.

"I'm lonely without you. Fanny's always out and so is Tip."

"I'm here now," Amy reassured him, spreading out a fresh tablecloth. She hated lying, but she had no choice if her father couldn't bear the truth. "I bought you a pint of port and some meat for supper."

As she began to cook, Fanny and Tip burst in.

"Have you washed my dress, Amy? Did you mend it?" asked Fanny.

"I want my clothes too," said Tip.

Amy produced two little bundles.

"Supper smells nice," they yawned, eyeing the food as though they expected it, like their clean clothes, as their right.

Chapter 2

Mother and son

Outside on the streets, rain fell in slanting lines. Thicker and faster it dropped, making mud swirl under a tide of wet umbrellas. Snug inside, in a coffee shop, Arthur Clennam downed his drink. He dreaded going home. He'd been abroad for ten years.

"Have you a room for the night?" he asked the waiter.

"Yup. Number seven's free. I'll show you the way."

Arthur stood up as if to follow the waiter and then shook his head. "Changed my mind," he said, his lips set in a resolute line. *I can't avoid my mother*, he thought, as he made his way to the shop that was also his home. *I have to tell her that Father's dead, even though she won't welcome me. She's never liked me.*

His childhood flooded back to him...

Every day, stern and hard, his mother had shoved her Bible in his face, snarling, "Wicked boy." He'd longed for her hugs, but they never came. Home had been a dark, unhappy place, as though it hid a secret.

It was still, he saw, as grim as ever, its bricks as black, its floorboards as creaky. It felt ramshackle, as though it might collapse at any moment.

He found his mother in a wheelchair. Her voice was cold. "Well, Arthur?" she snapped, flinching as he bent to kiss her.

"Mother! You can't walk?"

"Not for years. This room, from which I run the business, is my prison."

"I... I had no idea. Mother, I'm afraid I have some very bad news. Father is dead."

"Huh, that was no reason to return."

Shocked, he continued, "As Father lay dying, he gave me this watch. His last words were: 'For your mother.' He was so distressed… 'Put it right,' he kept saying. 'Put it right.' There are words engraved on the watch, too. DO NOT FORGET. What do they mean?"

"Nothing that concerns you."

It was only then that Arthur noticed a shabby girl sewing in a corner with quick, busy hands. She gave him a shy smile, before gathering her things and slipping quietly away.

"Who's that?"

"Little Dorrit. She does not concern you either."

"You haven't changed, Mother. When Father was alive, we did as you said. You ordered us abroad to help with the business. Now he's dead, you won't listen to me, so I'm leaving to strike out alone.

I don't want to make a fortune — money doesn't buy happiness — I'd just like to start afresh."

"Have you finished?" Mrs. Clennam asked.

"Not quite. Before he died, Father was full of guilt and remorse. Had he wronged anyone? If so, we could put it right. Will you help me discover the truth?"

"How dare you!" she spat. "In the first hour of your return, you insult your father's memory and ask me to spy on his transactions. Get out and don't come back. I'll hand over all our business dealings to Mr. Merdle. He's the biggest financier in London. I won't miss you."

All my life, thought Arthur, *however hard I tried, I never pleased her.* Finally, and sadly, he said goodbye.

As he left, he caught sight of Little Dorrit in the distance. *I'll catch up with her*, he thought. *My mother is hiding something and Little Dorrit may know what it is.*

Chapter 3

Who is Little Dorrit?

Arthur followed Little Dorrit through the street to a slum known as Bleeding Heart Yard. A ragged child ran up to her and grabbed her hand.

"Don't leave me!" cried the little girl.

"Oh Maggy, I can't stay," said Little Dorrit. "I have to get home."

"Who is she?" Arthur asked, coming up behind her.

"Oh! Mr. Clennam!" Amy uttered in surprise. "She's nobody's child. I feed her when I have anything to spare."

"You're my pretend ma," Maggy said.

Little Dorrit's a sewing maid and mother to street orphans, thought Arthur... *What else?*

"Why did you follow me?" Amy inquired. "I wish you had not."

"To ask you – what do you know of the House of Clennam?"

"Nothing… but Father might know. We live quite near, in the Marshalsea."

"The prison?" Arthur exclaimed.

"Don't judge him," said Amy, as they reached the Marshalsea gates. "He's unfortunate, not dishonest."

Inside his room, her father sat hunched, while her sister, Fanny, fastened a diamond bracelet to her wrist, put on a coat and hurried out. Amy was amazed. How could Fanny own such a treasure?

20

"This is Mr. Clennam, Father," she said, introducing Arthur.

"Welcome," said Mr. Dorrit, bowing. "Many visitors slip a token of their good will in my hand. Indeed, one particularly delicate gentleman wrapped two guineas inside a bunch of geraniums. For the Father of the Marshalsea. Not that I hint to you, sir."

"Father!" Amy groaned, agonized.

"Shh," he muttered, pocketing the coins Arthur discreetly handed him. "I do this for you."

"Do you know my family business, the House of Clennam, sir?" Arthur asked.

As Mr. Dorrit shook his head, the evening prison bell clanged. It was time for all visitors to leave.

"I'll show you out," said Amy. "I'm going out myself."

"Has your father many creditors still?" Arthur asked, on their way to the gate.

"Yes. Very many."

"Where can I find out about them? I could try to get him out of here."

"The Circumlocution Office holds the paperwork. But even if you could, would he cope with the change? Prison has broken him. How could he hold his head high in the world outside? People wouldn't respect him as they do here."

"I'll ask anyway," Arthur said. "I'd like to help."

"Tip!" exclaimed Amy, as her brother strolled inside the gate. "Why are you here? You live outside now. You have a job."

"Fired!" Tip grinned. "Didn't suit, like everything I've tried. Then I lost all my money on a horse. I'm banged up inside now, a debtor like Father."

"Oh," Amy cried. "I'll always love you, Tip, but if you can work, you should. Aren't you ashamed to be here?"

"I'm not rich, but maybe I can help Tip," said Arthur, catching Amy's worried glance as Tip walked away. "Where are you going, Little Dorrit?" he asked, to distract her.

"To my sister, Fanny. She's a dancer; she's rehearsing for a show." Amy nodded to the young jailor at the gate as she went through. "Goodnight, John."

"Goodnight, Little Dorrit," murmured John Chivery. "I'll wait up for you."

Arthur noticed his rapt look of adoration but missed Amy's indifference to it.

Leaving Amy, Arthur went in search of a place to stay. Now he'd left the family business, he'd have to find a new source of income. He wanted companionship too. He'd had a girlfriend, Flora, ten years ago, who was a widow now. He decided to look her up again. She'd been comfortably plump and far older than Little Dorrit.

Amy looked so young, even though she was the heart of her family. Was that, he wondered, why he wanted to help her... because, though small, she was such an extraordinary mixture of opposites, brave and vulnerable, tough and loving?

Chapter 4

Light and shadow

The playhouse where Fanny was rehearsing was down another alleyway. Amy pushed open the stage door to columns of dust and gaslight, a tinkling piano, dancing feet and swishing skirts.

A voice rapped out, "One, two, three... steady, darlings, one, two, three..."

Amy waited backstage in silence.

"Why are you here, you quiet little thing?" said Fanny, after the rehearsal.

"I wanted to ask about the bracelet."

"Oh, that. A gentleman gave it to me. I'm just going to see his mother. Come on, Amy, you can meet her."

She dragged Amy through the streets until they came to a row of grand houses where she rang the doorbell of the richest of them all.

"Is Mrs. Merdle at home?" Fanny demanded when the door was opened, sweeping past the butler and going in.

Mrs. Merdle, dripping with jewels, sat in a huge drawing room feeding a parrot perched in a golden cage.

"My sister, Amy," announced Fanny.

"Less showy than you, Miss Dorrit," Mrs. Merdle commented. "You've come because of my letter, I suppose. My son, Sparkler, wants to marry her," she explained to Amy, "but it's impossible. A second-rate dancer! Had she been an opera singer, I might have allowed it." She looked disgusted. "But a father in prison! No, Sparkler is made for better things."

The parrot squawked.

"Hush bird," said Mrs. Merdle.

"I propose," she continued to Fanny, "to give you such a large sum of money that you never come near my son again."

"Done!" said Fanny.

Mrs. Merdle fished out a bulky envelope and handed it over. "I never thought it would be so easy. We part friendly?"

"We certainly do," said Fanny.

Grinning broadly, she dragged Amy out into the street again.

"Don't you love Sparkler?" Amy asked.

"Not at all. He's stupid, but so rich..." Fanny's eyes shone with regret.

"Don't be hurt," Amy began cautiously, "but I don't think you should have taken Mrs. Merdle's money."

"She insulted me. A second-rate dancer, am I? Well, who made me a dancer? You! It's your fault. You're so meek and downtrodden... The only person who'll ever love you is that pathetic John Chivery. I'll always grab what I can. Someone's got to pull this family up."

Though Fanny's words hurt, Amy said nothing. It was pointless, arguing with your family. She only said, "I really don't love John."

Fanny flung her arms around Amy. "Poor little thing! I'm sorry. You were born in prison; you hardly understand anything. Trust me, I know how the world works."

Back in the dark, shadowy Marshalsea, Amy felt she was sinking into a trench she couldn't climb out of. Her father seized hold of her with a cry of relief.

I am in the shadows too, Amy thought, pouring him a drink. There's no escape. Fanny's right; I'm not clever or showy. I can only work for my family quietly, behind the scenes.

Chapter 5

Goodbye to the Marshalsea

Every day, while Amy sewed in Mrs. Clennam's house, Arthur Clennam went to the Circumlocution Office where he asked questions about Mr. Dorrit's affairs. There he met an inventor and engineer named Doyce.

"If only," Mr. Doyce sighed, "I had some money or could raise some. My invention is a winner."

"Tell me about it," said Arthur.

Arthur was so impressed by what he heard, that he invested all his money into it. Soon there was a new manufacturing firm, Doyce and Clennam, in Bleeding Heart Yard where Amy had told him people needed employment. The miserable alleyway was transformed into a prosperous street with working men and happy, healthy children instead of beggars and urchins.

Every evening, Arthur visited the Marshalsea to check Tip was working properly – he'd paid off Tip's debts and found him a job. When he visited, he had long talks with Little Dorrit and told her about Flora, his old girlfriend. "I loved her once. Could I do so again?" he wondered out loud. "Why do I talk to you like this?"

"Because you trust me?" said Amy. I trust him, she thought. He makes good things happen. I wish, I wish he loved me...

Arthur smiled at her clear eyes, but he was blind to the passion in her heart and deaf to her silent cry: I love you.

The next time Amy went to Bleeding Heart Yard, Maggy pleaded, "Tell me a story." With a sad smile on her face, Amy began...

Once, a Princess visited a tiny woman.

"Look," said the tiny woman. "I'll show you a secret." She opened a secret place and showed the Princess a shadow... someone who'd gone far away, never to come back.

"Why do you keep it?" asked the Princess.

"To remind me," the tiny woman replied. "No one so good has ever come here. When I die, the shadow will sink quietly into my grave, gone forever."

The next time the Princess visited the tiny woman, she was dead. The Princess peeped at the secret place, but the shadow had vanished. The tiny woman was right. The shadow had sunk into her grave, and she and it were at rest together...

"Is it true?" Maggy asked.

"Perhaps," whispered Amy, because her love for Arthur was like a shadow she'd hug to herself as long as she lived.

One evening, Arthur visited with startling news for the Dorrit family. "You're rich, Mr. Dorrit! I found papers proving it in the Circumlocution Office. You're heir to a huge fortune. That office is so crammed with lost paperwork, your lawyers never knew. In a few hours, you'll be free."

Mr. Dorrit stared unseeingly beyond the window, as though he couldn't imagine life outside.

"I m-must give presents to those who have been kind to us," stammered Mr. Dorrit. "The jailor for one... I must have new clothes too. I'll button up my coat for now. Ha! It looks broader, buttoned."

After the dressmakers, tailors and hatters had delivered their outfits, Tip ordered a carriage to whisk the family to a luxurious hotel. Prisoners cheered as they left. "Good luck to the Father of the Marshalsea!"

"Where's that tiresome Amy?" Fanny asked, waving from the carriage, her feathery hat billowing gracefully.

No one knew. They were all used to her being quietly where they wanted her.

"I see her," Tip said. "Being carried by Clennam. She should know better."

Amy lay in Arthur's arms, barely conscious.

"Take care of her," Arthur said, lifting her into the carriage. "She'd fainted in her bedroom. She must have gone there to change her dress and been overcome."

"That's what upsets me!" Fanny said. "Carried out, for everyone to see, in those dreadful, shabby clothes, when we look so stylish... She's disgraced us all. Father, tell the carriage to drive on."

Part Two: Riches

Chapter 6

Something wrong somewhere

Mr. Dorrit decided to take his family on a tour of Italy. "Pisa... Venice... canals, palaces, just the thing after — ahem — our old home. You girls must become ladies. Your new governess, Mrs. General, will teach you. Is that from Clennam?" he demanded, seeing Amy reading a letter.

"Yes, Father."

"Don't reply. We hardly knew him. He belongs to the past, which we must forget."

"But we know him well. And if it wasn't for Arthur..."

"I won't remember," Mr. Dorrit moaned, shuddering. So Amy took him to the balcony to see the view, and then went to fetch him a glass of wine.

"Sit down, Amy," complained Fanny. "You mustn't keep helping everyone. That's what the servants are for!"

Amy found this new life so much harder than the old one, and things grew even worse when the governess arrived.

"Father," sneered Mrs. General, "sounds so common. The word 'Papa' will give a pretty form to the lips. Say it before you enter a room... poultry, prunes, prisms, Papa."

"I'll try," Amy promised, but she kept forgetting.

"You hurt me," her father said. "I've suffered; I deserve my reward. Why can't you behave in your new role and sweep those terrible days away?"

"I will, Papa. I love you." Though she longed to make him happy, Amy felt she betrayed herself by never mentioning the past. I'm living a lie, she thought. I hate it.

Fanny and Tip adored their new life. Tip went racing again; Fanny went to parties.

"Guess who I met," she boasted to Amy. "Mr. and Mrs. Merdle and Sparkler! They're coming to see Papa. Mrs. Merdle wants me to marry her precious son now."

"Why?"

"Silly Amy!" Fanny unfurled her black and gold fan. "Because we're so rich."

Knowing none of the family felt the same about honesty and dignity, Amy was silent.

"I'll make them my slaves," Fanny giggled, as Amy wrote a last letter to Arthur.

Dear Arthur,

Italy's buildings are ancient and beautiful. In Pisa, the shadow of the leaning tower reminded me of the Marshalsea, when you were so kind and I was young. Though the tower is old, the earth and sky look young, like a promise of hope for a new tomorrow.

My family is happy, so here we stay. I...well, I never dreamed of wealth. Do not forget your grateful

Little Dorrit

Back in Bleeding Heart Yard, every word Arthur read brought Amy to his mind... He felt again her trust in him and her forlorn air of sweetness.

"When's Little Dorrit coming back?" Maggy asked him. "I want her."

"I don't know." Amy was gone; no good thinking about her. He decided instead to concentrate on the business. He'd invest with Mr. Merdle. Everyone knew Merdle was a financial genius, turning pennies into gold with a click of his fingers. After one visit to Mr. Merdle's office, the deed was done.

Chapter 7

Mr. Merdle's millions

"Delighted to welcome Fanny to the family," smirked Mrs. Merdle. "Such a sweet little heiress..."

"Indeed," bowed Mr. Dorrit, flattered. "I only wish I could invest my money as well as you."

"May I help?" said Mr. Merdle.

"Would you look after my money?"

"Delighted," smiled Mr. Merdle.

Very quickly, Mr. Merdle signed Mr. Dorrit's papers, promising to make his money grow. Mr. Dorrit glowed. He was accepted, rich, and almost related to the famous Merdle family.

The Merdles held a wedding reception for Fanny in their Venetian palace, inviting dukes, duchesses, princes and princesses. Yes, the bad times were over...

But at the party Mr. Dorrit felt ill. The long table dazzled him, shining with silver and glass; conversation buzzed, confusing him. Past and present merged into one...

Rising, he announced into a horrified silence, "My friends... Welcome to the Marshalsea Prison! You may find it uncomfortable... but you'll get used to it as I did. I am the Father of the Marshalsea.

Out of respect for my position, many
people offer – little tributes – which
I accept for my child's
sake... Amy, born here,
child of an unfortunate
father... God bless
you all." And
he collapsed,
sobbing.

Tip and Fanny were horrified. Amy
wasn't in the least ashamed, only anxious
to get him quickly home to bed.

Within two weeks, Mr. Dorrit was dead.

By then, Fanny and Sparkler had already
departed for their grand London house.

"It's such a bore," Fanny raged. "Just
when I pictured myself shining in society
in my lovely new dresses, I'm wearing
horrible black mourning clothes. Amy
must stay with us. It'll cheer me up."

Amy agreed. She had nowhere else to go. Back in London, she went to visit Mrs. Clennam.

"I miss you, Little Dorrit," Mrs. Clennam said, "though I'm glad you're rich now."

"It hasn't brought me much happiness," Amy sighed. "How is Arthur?"

"Never see him," Mrs. Clennam snapped. She didn't mention that she'd banned him from her house.

Arthur was busy searching for clues about his father's watch with its message, DO NOT FORGET.

He found the answer at last in a will, buried in the Circumlocution Office – his grandfather's will. He read it with amazement and disbelief. Then he went to his mother.

"This says..." he showed it to her, "my grandfather left a fortune to Little Dorrit! It says my father, though married to you, had an affair with another woman, named Lizzy. It says you took the child of that affair, and that Lizzy, deprived of her baby, died of a broken heart in Marshalsea Prison. Before she died she wrote to my grandfather, and he, sorry for her suffering, left his fortune to the next child to be born at the prison – Amy Dorrit!"

"After I warned you to stay out of it, how dare you pry..." hissed Mrs. Clennam.

"You never gave the money to Amy. He had that watch engraved to remind you. Do not forget, Mother. DO NOT FORGET. What happened to the child?"

"Don't you understand?" she muttered. "It was you... Born in sin to a wicked woman. I had no children... I wanted a child. I was always strict with you, to stop you from growing up like your mother."

Arthur, stunned, stammered, "I-I know you never liked me..." He controlled himself. "You must tell Amy. Give her the money."

"The shame... No... I can't confess it now. Let the truth lie buried as before."

"You are hard, Mother, but not lacking in courage. Do what is right."

Leaving her, he went to Bleeding Heart Yard. Mr. Doyce, his partner, was anxious.

"Have you heard? Mr. Merdle, the great financier, is a crook! Everyone who let him invest their money has lost it."

"Oh no," said Arthur, cold to his very bones. "He's got this firm's money. If it's true, we're in debt. Though the firm is doing well, we owe thousands. It's my fault. I'll take the blame."

Arthur's fear was justified. He was arrested for debt and sentenced to the Marshalsea prison.

"I remember you," said John Chivery, the jailor, as Arthur was brought in. "You visited Mr. Dorrit. My father, Bob, was jailor here when Amy was born. And for Amy's sake, I'll treat you well."

Arthur shivered. He felt stupefied... ill... as though nothing mattered now. He knew that prison, with no chance of release, had smeared his existence in shame and disgrace.

"I loved Amy," John was saying, bitterly, "but she wouldn't look at me. Do you know why? No, you never cared. She loved you, Mr. Clennam, not me. You were blind and deaf to her, and I suffered because of you."

"Amy loved... me?"

John nodded, wiping away his tears.

"I've been so stupid," muttered Arthur, "...too late, now..." He threw himself onto his hard prison bed, ice cold, though his skin felt on fire. He closed his eyes. Fever had seized him in its cruel claws, and dragged him out of consciousness into a nightmare of delirium.

Chapter 8

The end makes
a beginning

M r. Merdle strolled to Fanny and
Sparkler's house. He knew that the
City was after him. He'd lost millions –
handed over by friends and strangers, rich
and poor alike – all gambled and gone.
His financial empire, built on his lies and

trickery, had collapsed. Well, it was good while it lasted, but now it was over. Play it cool, he told himself.

"Charmed, I'm sure, Papa-in-law," said Fanny, when he came in.

"Could you lend me a pocketknife, my dear?"

"Sparkler," ordered Fanny. "Get the mother-of-pearl pocketknife out of my workbox."

"I'd prefer one with a darker handle," said Mr. Merdle.

"Tortoise-shell?"

"Thank you. You shall have it back tomorrow."

That was his last lie. The following day, the pocketknife was held by the police, its dark handle stained red with blood. Mr. Merdle had cut his throat with it, to avoid capture, to avoid a trial, to avoid justice, to avoid truth.

He had not even protected his family from his wrong-doing.

"I can't believe Pa-in-law left us nothing!" wailed Fanny. "How could you let it happen, Sparkler? Mrs. Merdle?"

"Don't speak like that. I'm a grieving widow, disgracefully deceived!" snapped Mrs. Merdle.

Fighting made them feel better, and because Mrs. Merdle wouldn't leave Sparkler and Sparkler wouldn't leave Fanny, for the rest of their days they lived together, squabbling and snapping, joined by Tip who always moaned about the bad luck life had dealt him.

"Merdle's ruined me," spat Mrs. Clennam. "Meanwhile, I hear Arthur's business is improving, even though he's in prison for debt."

Amy, visiting her, tried to give comfort. "You were kind to me, when I sewed here. What can I do for you?"

"Kind? No..." Pale with shame, Mrs. Clennam picked up the old will. "Read this."

Amy read quickly. When she looked up, Mrs. Clennam had fallen out of the wheelchair onto her knees, her mouth twisted in agony, her arms outstretched.

"Don't," said Amy. "You are too old to kneel to me. The money means nothing. I never wanted wealth. I forgive you freely."

"I think you love Arthur," said Mrs. Clennam. "I've been hard on him because religion teaches us to set ourselves against doing evil... like his mother."

"I believe," Amy replied steadily, "that true religion teaches not vengeance or suffering, but love."

There was silence. Then an ominous clatter... a rumble... a falling down...

Quickly, Amy dragged Mrs. Clennam outside – just in time. The old house rocked, broke and collapsed in a whirlwind of dust. All that remained was a heap of tumbled fragments. The shock was too much for Mrs. Clennam's feeble health. She fell forward onto the stones, beyond help, lifeless.

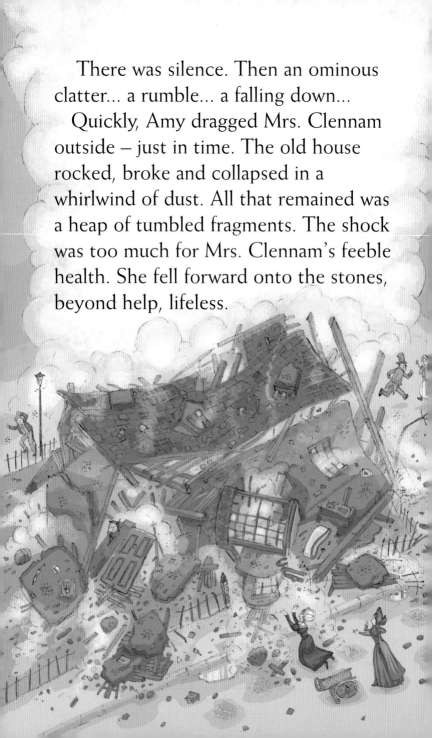

Stumbling over the ruins, Amy ran to the Marshalsea. It seemed like old times, going there, but this time she had to tell Arthur about his mother. She found him raging with fever and though day after day she fed him, soothed him, washed him, he never recognized his nurse.

He dreamed of Amy smiling at him as he lay in bed.

"Is it truly you?" he whispered at last, unable to distinguish between dreaming and reality. "My own Little Dorrit?"

"Truly me," she whispered back. "Don't you know I love you?"

"I love you too. I always have, though I didn't know it. But I can't leave this prison. I can't marry you..."

"Dearest Arthur, there is money for your release." Her inheritance from the hidden will would pay off the debts.

"I can't take your fortune."

Amy thought quickly. She couldn't bear to wound his pride. She'd pay, she decided, and never tell.

"I haven't any," she laughed. "Nothing left! Merdle lost it all, but your business has been doing well. You can get yourself out of here."

"Dear Amy," said Arthur, amazed how light the room felt, full of joy.

And when they married, the sun beamed its rays upon them as the church bells pealed a round of glorious noise. They walked quietly into the roaring streets among the jostling, eager crowds, their hands clasped together... happy, inseparable and blessed.

Charles Dickens 1812-1870

Charles Dickens lived in London, England, during the reign of Queen Victoria. When he was twelve, his father was sent to the Marshalsea Debtors' Prison. The rest of the family moved in too, apart from Dickens, who had to find lodgings in the city's slums. He hated it and never forgot how hard life could be for the poor.

Dickens went on to become one of the most famous writers of his time, highlighting in his novels the unfair nature of Victorian society, with its vast gulf between rich and poor. His other tales include *Oliver Twist*, *Great Expectations*, *A Christmas Carol*, *A Tale of Two Cities*, *Bleak House* and *David Copperfield*.

Usborne Quicklinks
To find out more about Dickens and life in Victorian times, go to the Usborne Quicklinks Website at www.usborne-quicklinks.com Read the internet safety guidelines, and then type the keywords "Little Dorrit".